W9-ABB-386

Jeremy McBright
Was Afraid of the Night

Jeremy McBright Was Afraid of the Night

By William Bradford

CyPress Publications

Tallahassee, Florida

Inquiries should be addressed to:

CyPress Publications

P.O. Box 2636

Tallahassee, Florida 32316-2636

http://cypress-starpublications.com

lraymond@nettally.com

Library of Congress Cataloging-in-Publication Data

Bradford, William, 1957-
Jeremy McBright was afraid of the night / by William Bradford.
    p. cm.
  Summary: After asking Jeremy to show him the creatures that make him afraid at bed time, his father helps Jeremy to appreciate the night.
  ISBN-13: 978-0-9672585-2-2
  [1. Fear of the dark—Fiction. 2. Night—Fiction. 3. Fathers and sons—Fiction. 4. Bed time—Fiction. 5. Stories in rhyme.] I. Title.
  PZ8.3.B72297Jer 2006
  [E]—dc22
  2005028362

ISBN 10 0-9672585-2-9

ISBN 13 978-0-9672585-2-2

First Edition

Dedication

To Rebecca and Sydney, creators of proud parents

Jeremy McBright was afraid of the night.
The daytime was great, but the dark was a fright.

The scariest time was when Jeremy went to bed.
There were spooks underneath him and ghosts overhead.

Afraid of his closet, he kept the door closed,
and covered up with blankets from his nose to his toes.

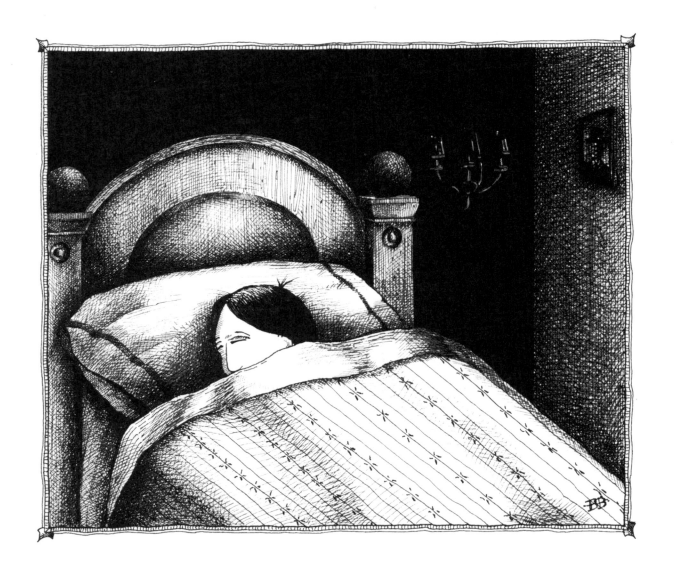

Finally, after much tossing and turning around,
he'd fall off to sleep hardly making a sound.

In the morning he'd wake to the happy sunlight,
with no spooks around him and no need for fright.

But he knew that the nighttime would follow the day,
and again he'd be scared in his usual way.

One evening at supper with his mom and his dad
he explained to his father the fear that he had.

His dad listened, then took him upstairs to his room,
and asked Jeremy to show him the creatures of doom.

"They only come out when it's dark," Jeremy said.
So they turned the lights off and sat down on his bed.

9

The young boy knelt down and peeked under his bed,
his dad right beside him, the two head to head.

But all that was under his small wooden bed
were a few balls of dust and a spool of Mom's thread.

They walked to the closet to see what was there.
There were sneakers, shirts, pants, and a stuffed teddy bear.

They looked for the arm he was sure he could see.
It was just a dead branch from an old maple tree.

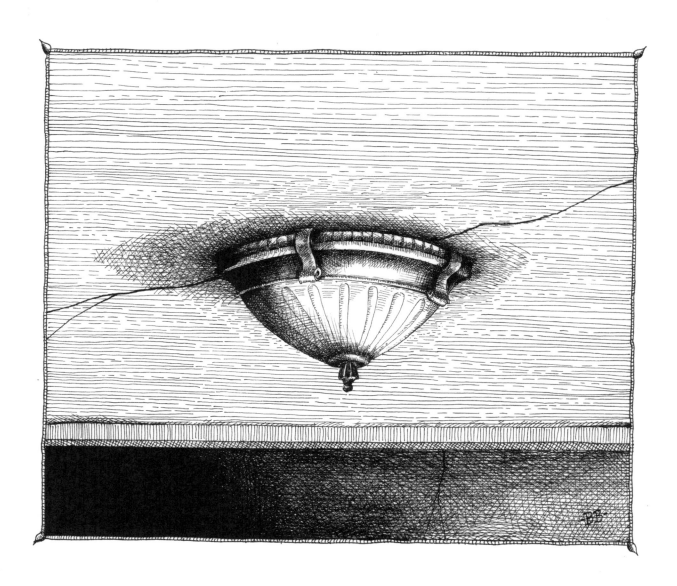

They looked overhead where ghosts floated at night.
But all that was there was a brass ceiling light.

They finished their search and then walked down the stairs,
went into the den and sat down in two chairs.

"Jeremy," his father began with a wink,
"we'd really miss the nighttime if we stop and we think.

"Why, we wouldn't see fireworks on the Fourth of July.
No starlight, or moonlight, they'd all pass us by.

"We couldn't see fireflies or enjoy trick-or-treat,
and the jack-o-lantern pumpkins that light up our street.

"You'd miss the warm fireplace in winter, I bet,
when the night air is chilly, or did you forget?

"At Christmas, bright tree lights would not mean a thing.
And no nighttime in summer means crickets won't sing.

"But of all the good things maybe this one is best,
night is the time for a tired world to rest."

21

He smiled at his son and then patted his head.
Jeremy hugged his wise father and went upstairs to bed.

22

Strangely, all that seemed scary just one night before
did not seem so spooky or strange anymore.

Jeremy McBright who once dreaded the night,
learned that nighttime, like daytime, was filled with delight.

The End

Other Children's Books
Published by
CyPress
Publications

Orion the Skateboard Kid, by Juanita S. Raymond and Leland F. Raymond. ISBN 0-9672585-0-2, 63 pages, $9.95
—*Enthusiastically recommended for school and community library collections* Orion The Skateboard Kid *is entertaining, engaging reading for 4th and 5th grade level students.* —Midwest Book Review, "Children's Bookwatch," December 2001

Sarah and the Sand Dollar, by Kathie L. Underwood. ISBN 0-9672585-7-X, 36 pages, $11.95
This book, *Sarah and the Sand Dollar,* is based on a true story. While fishing in the Apalachicola Bay, off the coast of Florida, Kathie Underwood experienced the miracle of the sand dollar. Now, inspired by God, she has written her story for children, so they may learn of His abundant love for us.

The Smallest Toy Store, by Regina N. Lewis, illustrated by P.M. Moore. ISBN 0-9672585-8-8, 44 pages, $12.95
—*The holiday is Christmas, the day children dream about all year as they imagine gifts with their names on them. In her charmingly illustrated new book,* The Smallest Toy Store, *Regina Lewis gently reminds her readers that there are children who face the holiday, and every day, without a place to call home, much less a tree or presents. Join the magical Ms. MerryWood and celebrate the true meaning of Christmas."* —Adrian Fogelin, *author* Crossing Jordan, Anna Casey's Place in the World, My Brother's Hero, Sister Spider Knows All, *and* The Big Nothing

Visit our website for ordering information and news of upcoming titles.
http://cypress-starpublications.com

CyPress Publications

PO Box 2636
Tallahassee, FL, 32316-2636
Voice: (850) 576-8820
Fax: (850) 576-9968
lraymond@nettally.com
http://cypress-starpublications.com

To order copies of *Jeremy McBright was Afraid of the Night* by mail, please fill out the information below and mail to the address above. Please include check or money order in the amount of $19.00 ($13.95 + $1.05 tax + $4.00 shipping and handling) made out to CyPress Publications.

Name _____

Address _____

Phone _____

E-mail _____

Thank You for your Order!

Visit our website for ordering information and news of upcoming titles.
http://cypress-starpublications.com